To Primrose, who has no fear.

The Listening Walk

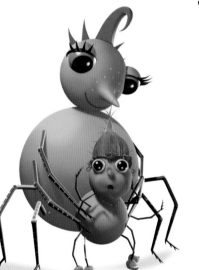

By David Kirk

Callaway

New York 2005

Tucking all her children in, Miss Spider dimmed the light.
She listened to the summer sounds, the soothing songs of night.
The children dreamt of honey drops and gleaming streams of dew,
Of soaring to the soft, white clouds—of drifting gently through.

Eight buggy babies safe in bed—with seven fast asleep.

But little Wiggle lay awake, too terrified to peep.

Hoots and toots and tweets and twitters swirled around his head.

Surrounded by those soft, sweet sounds, he heard these things instead . . .

The creaking bones of creeping beasts that prowled the twisted trees,
The shrieks and moans of buggies begging bent upon their knees.
Wiggle hid beneath his sheets—his eyes were bugging wide.
Gnawing, gnashing monster teeth clacked greedily outside!

Racing to his parents' room, he dove into their bed.
Miss Spider sat up with a start. "What now?" his father said.
"Just listen," Wiggle whispered, "and you'll hear the monsters, too.
They're lurking in the trees out there. May I squeeze in with you?"

"It's bugaboos!" Miss Spider said. "Your mom knows just the cure!
A listening walk is all you need—a nighttime forest tour."
So out into the lively night she led her frightened son,
To place a face to every sound that spooked the little one.

Poor Wiggle jumped and jittered when he heard a *clack clack clack*.
But it was only Eunice Earwig crunching down a snack.
"Well that one's not so bad," he said, "but I heard other sounds
I'm sure were fearsome monster beasties prowling on their rounds."

Just up ahead a *creaking*, *creaking* rocked a tiny tree.
Miss Spider pulled her Wiggle very close so he could see.
She said, "It's not a monster, dear; Spindella is our friend."
"I'm sure the monsters," Wiggle sniffed, "are slithering 'round the bend."

Then overhead a *whooshing* made poor Wiggle jump and squeal.
"They're swooping down to get me. I don't want to be a meal!"
But it was only Louie Luna looping through the sky.
"I guess he's not so scary," Wiggle sniffled with a sigh.

"It's funny," Wiggle giggled, "night's not spooky like I thought—
With monsters hiding everywhere, 'cause now I see they're not.
I don't believe in monsters. Now there's nothing more to dread.
I'm absolutely sure my nighttime bugaboos have fled!"

He smiled up at his mother, then gazed into the air,
Imagining the beasties that he knew were never there.
A thousand phosphorescent eyes were blinking from the trees . . .

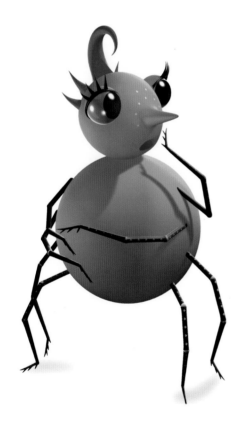

"I do believe in monsters!" Wiggle croaked. "Don't eat me, please!"

"They're only fireflies!" laughed his mom. "We've come along this way
To get our chance to see them dance the firefly ballet."
They sat together on a leaf, the forest all aglow,
And watched the swirling magic of the brilliant midnight show.

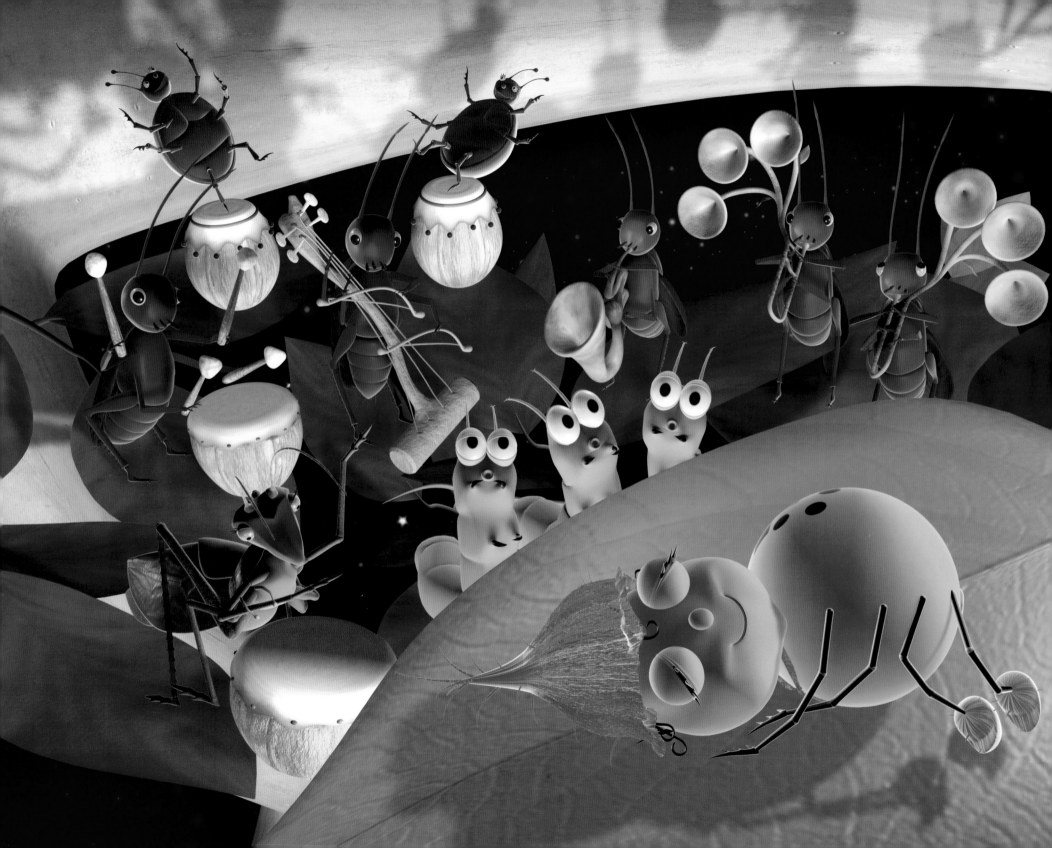

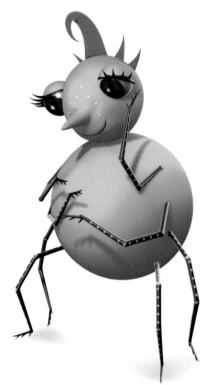

"The night is pretty," Wiggle yawned, "and quite a lot of fun.
But still, I'm glad we get to live and play out in the sun."
They climbed into the Cozy Hole and Wiggle fell in bed.
The melodies of evening made a pillow for his head.

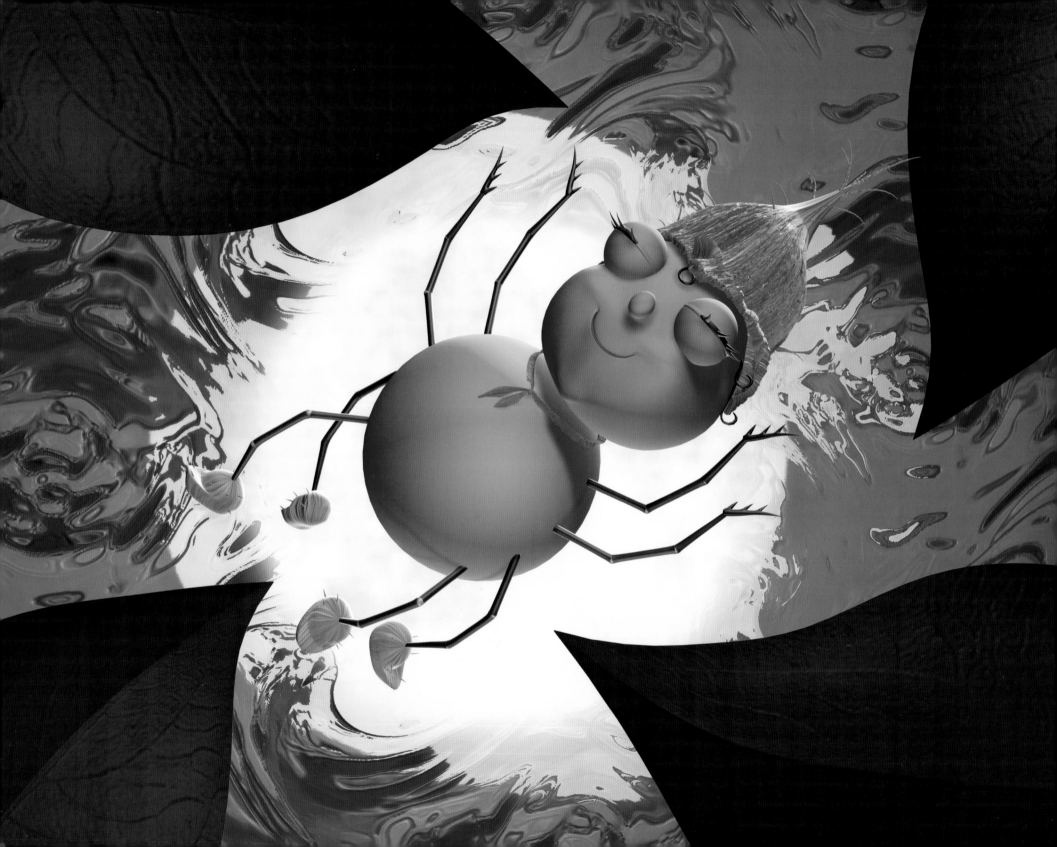

And in another moment he had drifted into sleep,
Swimming gently through the music of the friendly forest deep.

This book is based on the TV episode "The Listening Walk," written by Nadine Van Der Velde, from the animated TV series *Miss Spider's Sunny Patch Friends* on Nick Jr., a Nelvana Limited/Absolute Pictures Limited co-production in association with Callaway Arts & Entertainment, based on the Miss Spider books by David Kirk.

Nicholas Callaway, President and Publisher
Cathy Ferrara, Managing Editor and Production Director
Toshiya Masuda, Art Director • Nelson Gomez, Director of Digital Technology
Joya Rajadhyaksha, Associate Editor • Amy Cloud, Associate Editor • Doug Vitarelli, Director of Animation
Alex Ballas, Assistant Designer • Raphael Shea, Art Assistant • Krupa Jhaveri, Design Assistant
Cara Paul, Digital Artist • Aharon Charnov, Digital Artist • Masako Ebata, Designer

Special thanks to the Nelvana staff, including Doug Murphy, Scott Dyer, Tracy Ewing, Pam Lehn,
Tonya Lindo, Susie Grondin, Luis Lopez, Eric Pentz, and Georgina Robinson.

Cover digital art by Mark Picard.

Library of Congress Cataloging-in-Publication Data available upon request.

Distributed in the United States by Viking Children's Books.

Callaway Arts & Entertainment, its Callaway logotype, and Callaway & Kirk Company LLC are trademarks.

Visit Callaway Arts & Entertainment at www.callaway.com

ISBN 0-448-43999-9

10 9 8 7 6 5 4 3 2 1   05 06 07 08 09 10

First edition, September 2005

Printed in China by Oro Editions - Max Production

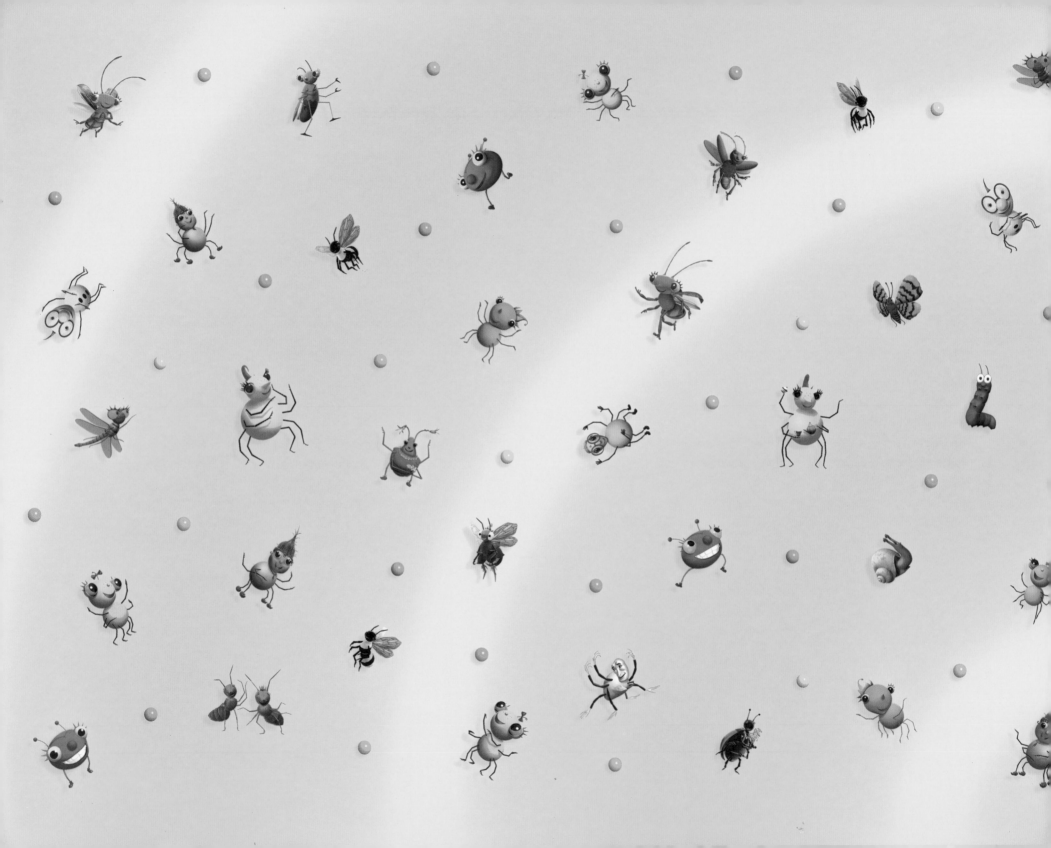